Judith Caseley

JORAH'S JOURNAL

 GREENWILLOW BOOKS, NEW YORK

For Mrs. Humphrey and Dr. Wooten,
who gave Michael and Jenna a joyous first
year at Glenwood Landing School

The preseparated two-color art was prepared with
a combination of pen-and-ink line and watercolor.
The text type is Kuenstler 480 Roman.
Printed in the United States of America
First Edition 10 9 8 7 6 5 4 3 2 1

Library of Congress Cataloging-in-Publication Data
Caseley, Judith.
Jorah's journal / by Judith Caseley.
p.   cm.
Summary: In her new journal, Jorah records her feelings about
having to move, going to a new school, celebrating her birthday,
learning the meaning of her name, and finding a friend.
ISBN 0-688-14879-4 [1. Moving, Household—Fiction.
2. Diaries—Fiction.]   I. Title.   PZ7.C2677Jo   1997
[Fic]—dc20   96-10411   CIP   AC

CONTENTS

1

MOVING DAY.........1

2

THE NEW GIRL
IN CLASS.........16

3

JORAH'S LESSON.........28

4

JORAH AND CALEB.........38

5

JORAH'S BIRTHDAY.........49

CHAPTER 1
MOVING DAY

Jorah sat on the floor of her bedroom, listening to the sound of the rain as it pattered against the air conditioner.

Ordinarily Jorah loved the rain. She loved dancing in the puddles, catching raindrops on her tongue, and singing at the top of her lungs as the wind whistled around her. But on this rainy day in September she didn't dance or sing or catch raindrops on her tongue. On this rainy day in September Jorah and her family were moving.

Jorah had never heard the sound of the rain on the rooftop because she and her family lived on the second floor of an apartment building. Her best friend, Sami, had been to the rooftop to see the pigeons nesting there and had promised to take Jorah someday.

Tears trickled down Jorah's face as she realized that she would never get to see the top of the building, and that she would never again see the playground, where she and Sami had ridden their bicycles, or the fifth floor, where Sami lived.

Jorah felt as though they had been moving forever. It had started with whispering between her parents, with lots of secret talk and telephone calls and

worried looks going on, until one day Jorah's father announced that he had gotten a new job in a city about two hours away.

"At first we thought that your father might commute," Mama said.

"What's 'commute' mean?" Jorah's brother, Caleb, asked.

"It's when you go back and forth to a place every day," Papa replied.

"Soon I'm going to commute to kindergarten," said Caleb.

Jorah started laughing, but her parents were looking much too serious for laughter, and she closed her mouth quickly.

Papa continued. "I drove there one morning, and it was just too far."

Mama cleared her throat and said, "That's why we have to move," so quietly that Jorah could hardly believe her ears.

Caleb had gone on playing with his action figures until Jorah snatched the fiercest warrior away from him, saying, "Don't you realize what this means? No more Danny and no more playground and no more Joe in the wheelchair and no more anything or anybody that we know."

"That's okay," was Caleb's reply, and Mama had started to laugh, but Jorah didn't think it was funny at all. Not one bit funny.

This rainy day in September Jorah stared at her faded wallpaper. A smudged gray rectangle marked the place where her framed princess poster had hung.

The room was no longer cluttered with her toys mixed in with Caleb's: building blocks and stuffed animals and board games and books. Jorah sat in the middle of an empty room.

"It's time to go, Jorah," said her mother from the doorway.

Jorah pushed herself up from the floor
and moved toward the window, kissing her
fingers and touching them to one wall.
Then she did the same to the three other
walls as her mother watched.

Caleb ran into the room shouting,
"Good-bye!" so cheerfully that Jorah felt
like smacking him.

"It's good-bye forever," she told Caleb,
but Caleb zoomed out of the room.

The moving men were wet and unhappy as they carried Mama's flowered armchair out of the apartment, down the hallway to the elevator, and out into the rain. Jorah's mother walked behind them, worrying that the chair would get wet.

Thunder started, and Caleb began to cry. Papa carried him to the car, even though Caleb was a big boy for his age and Papa already had hurt his back trying to move furniture.

Jorah followed slowly behind, thinking it might be nice to be carried out the door of her old apartment like a baby.

The moving van followed Jorah and her family in their car as they drove onto the highway in the pouring rain.

By the time the movers had unloaded the furniture and fifty-two boxes and bags of clothes and cartons of shoes and three large potted plants into the house,

everybody looked as gloomy as the weather.

"You won't be crowded anymore," said Mama softly as she and Papa showed Jorah her new room.

"It was cozy sharing with Caleb," said Jorah.

"You'll make new friends," Papa told her, pointing out the window at a little girl in a blue rain slicker, twirling a big daisy umbrella.

"She looks weird," said Jorah, peering out the window. "I want my old friends. I want Sami."

"We have a big backyard to play in," said Caleb.

"I miss our old playground," said Jorah.

Jorah's mother gave each of the children a package wrapped in pretty paper. "It's a housewarming gift," explained Mama.

"Is it a heater?" asked Caleb.

Mama laughed. "A housewarming gift is a present that you give someone to say 'Welcome to your new home,'" she said.

Jorah and Caleb opened their packages. Jorah's present was a book with blank pages in it, and on the cover Mama had written, "Jorah's Journal."

"Write whatever you like," said her mother. "It's your own private notebook."

Caleb held up his present. "It's my own private coloring book," he said.

That first night in her new room Jorah sat down at her desk. Her mother had bought Jorah a new lamp, and the ceiling light and newly painted walls made the room look bright and cozy. Jorah looked around.

Mama had unpacked several boxes and tried to cluster Jorah's menagerie of dolls and animals in exactly the same way that Jorah had arranged them in her old bedroom: bears and rabbits against one pillow, dolls against another, and whatever was left over against a third pillow, a wall of dolls and animals that would welcome her to bed. Mama had tried hard.

Jorah examined her clean white walls. Perhaps the princess poster would look nice hanging above the animals, she thought. The walls were empty now, except for a brown smudge near her closet. Had the painters missed a spot?

Jorah peered more closely. Suddenly the spot moved so quickly that she wondered if she had imagined it, until it appeared again on her closet door.

"Papa!" cried Jorah. "Help!"

Caleb came running and would have pounced on the brown spot himself if Jorah hadn't stopped him.

"I think it's a spider," she told her brother, "and it's the fastest spider I ever saw, and I don't want it to get away."

"Papa!" cried Caleb. "A huge spider!"

"A huge, fast spider!" cried Jorah.

Papa arrived with a newspaper, and

Mama ran after him with a jar and a lid. "Don't squish that spider all over Jorah's clean white walls," she told him.

Papa tiptoed closer to the insect. "That's not a spider," he whispered. "That's a cricket!"

"Get rid of the cricket," whispered Jorah, but Caleb hopped the way he thought a cricket would hop, and the cricket flew along the wall and disappeared.

"Sorry," said Papa.

"We'll get it next time," said Mama.

"He's faster than me," said Caleb as they all left Jorah's bedroom.

Jorah sat down at her desk again. She examined the walls carefully. Then she picked up her felt-tipped pen, opened up her journal, and wrote quickly:

My name is Jorah.
I'm in my new bedroom now, and I'm not alone. This place has crickets. My old house didn't have any bugs at all, except maybe a few ants in the summer. But ants aren't big and gross. Crickets are. I hate it here.
Good night.

yuck!

Jorah got into bed, pulled the covers up to her chin, and checked the walls one last time to see if any more crickets were lurking. She was thankful that the room was bright and well lit. The walls were clean and white and empty.

Jorah pulled the covers over her head and fell asleep with all the lights burning, despite the fact that her mother had warned Caleb and her not to waste electricity.

CHAPTER 2
THE NEW GIRL IN CLASS

On the morning of the first day of school, Jorah's knees felt like jelly. The waffle her mother made her, dripping with syrup the way she liked it, would barely go down.

Caleb was still hopping around like a cricket, full of excitement because he had heard that the kindergarten in his new school had ducklings and rabbits.

Watching her brother, Jorah felt a stab of jealousy. Kindergarten wasn't scary at all. Jorah wished that she could color with crayons again, build skyscrapers out of blocks again, study squirrels again, and have rest time on a little mat again, just like Caleb.

Mama drove Jorah and Caleb to school. "Tomorrow," she told them, "you'll take the school bus. Today I'll get you settled."

Caleb was jumpy with anticipation. Jorah dragged her feet, not quite hard enough to do damage to the new pair of green loafers with a green feather on each shoe that she had begged her mother to buy her. They were absolutely the coolest shoes in the world, she had told Mama, mustering up her finest pleading look until Mama had agreed.

As soon as she had waved good-bye to Mama and climbed the gray steps to the second floor and found classroom number eight, eyes on her green shoes every step of the way, she knew that the green-feathered loafers were a big mistake.

"Weird shoes," said a loud voice, and Jorah's eyes met the brown, cocker-spaniel eyes of a girl with a head full of black, curly ringlets. "Weird feathers," the girl added, turning up the volume.

"Weird feathers" and "New girl" and "Maybe they wear green shoes where she comes from" filled the classroom until a small, pretty woman walked briskly to the front of the room, announcing, "Most of you know that my name is Mrs. Postal. Let's go around the room and introduce ourselves."

The girl who had made fun of her shoes

sat a mere two seats away. Jorah's heart beat wildly as the girl introduced herself.

"My name is Mora, and everybody knows me, except for the new girl," said Mora, jabbing a finger past her neighbor toward Jorah.

"My name is Jay," said a blond boy with bangs that flicked as he blinked his eyes. "And the new girl's shoes remind me of what happens at the bottom of my canary's cage."

The whole class hooted, at least to Jorah's ears they did, until Mrs. Postal said,

"They're such a pretty green. They go well with your hair, Jay."

The class hooted some more, with Jay shaking his head, making his fine bangs fly back and forth, and then it was Jorah's turn.

"My name is Jorah, and I'm new," squeaked Jorah, turning pink at the sound of her own voice.

"Welcome to Glen Forest School," said Mrs. Postal. "I know you'll make lots of new friends."

Jorah was not at all convinced, but she got through the morning, sorting out seating assignments and math books and spelling notebooks.

As Jorah stood in line for lunch, eyes fixed on her shoes, she felt as though the small green feathers had grown into Dr. Seuss–like plumes.

The cafeteria was noisy and crowded as the children who had brought their lunches took their seats.

Jorah watched a girl named Kerry, with braids that reminded her of Pippi Longstocking's, trade cookies with a girl

named Ginger. Ginger had red hair and chocolate-covered graham crackers, which Jorah liked much more than the boring fig cookies that her mother had packed.

Ginger smiled at Jorah and said, "We have a doll club," but she said nothing to

Jorah about joining it. "Would you like a cookie?" she added, holding out a chocolate-covered graham cracker.

Just as Jorah smiled and reached for her first real treat of the day, she felt a hard yank at the back of her head. Her head tipped back, and a cackling Jay jeered over her shoulder as the cookie smashed to the floor.

"He's crazy," said Ginger, shaking her head. "I don't have any more cookies, though."

"It's okay," said Jorah, blinking back tears as she smoothed her hair. "I have my fig bars. Would anyone like one?" she asked.

Kerry said, "No, thank you," and Melissa stuck her fingers in her mouth, sideways, as if she were going to gag. Jorah got the point. Very soon after that, lunch was over.

Mama picked the children up at school, but Jorah moped all the way home. To her surprise, so did Caleb.

Mama seemed more concerned with his sad face than with Jorah's. "How was your first day at kindergarten, Caleb?" she asked brightly.

"Not good," said Caleb. "I like my old world better."

"Your old world?" said Mama, trying not to smile.

"My new world smells," Caleb explained.

Jorah couldn't help asking. "What smells?" she said.

"The place where we eat lunch. It smells bad." Caleb hung his head. "I never want to eat there again."

"He means the cafeteria!" said Jorah. "It smells like mustard," she told Mama. "Today was hot dog day."

"Hot dogs smell," said Caleb, holding his nose.

"You'll get used to it," said Mama.

"I won't," said Caleb, plugging his ears.

"I need better cookies to trade," said Jorah. "Nobody wants fig bars."

Before Mama could answer, Caleb burst into tears. "There were no ducklings or rabbits!" he wailed, covering his face with his hands.

"Oh, dear," said Mama, hugging Caleb. "Maybe we have to wait until springtime."

"What about my cookies?" insisted Jorah.

"For heaven's sake," Mama said crossly. "Fig cookies are just fine."

That night after supper Jorah sat down

at her desk and opened her journal. She examined her wall for crickets. There were none. Then she wrote:

Today I went to my new school. Kerry looks nice, but her best friend is Ginger. Ginger has red hair. They have a doll club. I'm not invited. Ginger gave me a cookie. A boy named Jay pulled my hair and it broke. My cookie, not my hair. A girl named Mora made fun of my shoes. Fig bars are yucky. So is school. There are no crickets there. Just Mora and Jay. Caleb likes our old world better, and so do I.

CHAPTER 3
JORAH'S LESSON

The next morning Jorah ate her usual waffle for breakfast.

Caleb refused to eat at all. He shook his head at scrambled eggs, cornflakes, toast, and even pancakes, which his mother normally made only on weekends.

"Try to eat something," pleaded Mama.

"How about a waffle?" said Jorah, glad

for the distraction because maybe now her mother wouldn't notice that Jorah wasn't wearing her new green shoes.

"I'm full," said Caleb, sitting on the floor and driving his dump truck around the carpet.

Jorah had almost made it out the front door in her sneakers when her mother said, "Jorah, you don't have gym today, do you? We bought your new green shoes to go with that outfit."

"I can't wear my green shoes at this school," said Jorah.

But Mama had already found the green shoes in the back of Jorah's closet. "Nonsense," she said, removing Jorah's sneakers and slipping the loafers on her feet. "They're adorable." She turned toward Caleb. "Let's go, honey," said Mama. "If we don't hurry, we'll miss the school bus."

Mama walked Jorah and Caleb to the bus stop, and they joined a group of children waiting there.

Jorah spied a familiar head of black, curly hair as Mora crossed the street and took her place behind Jorah.

"You're tall," said Mora, looking up at Jorah as if she were looking up at a tall building. "Do those green shoes have high heels or something?"

Caleb eyed Mora. "Look, Mama, I'm almost as big as she is," he announced.

"Introduce me to your new friend, Jorah," Mama said hastily.

Before Jorah could say a word, Mora replied, "I'm Mora. I don't live very far from here. See? That's my mother waving." Mora waved back at a lady standing in the doorway of a yellow house across the street.

"Your house is yellow," said Caleb. "I wanted my house to be yellow."

"What color is your house?" Mora asked. "It's not green with feathers, is it?" she added, laughing.

"It's white," said Jorah coldly. Then she took Caleb's hand, and they boarded the bus.

"Good-bye!" called Mama from the sidewalk. "Have a great day!"

Jorah slid down next to her brother, who already sat slumped in his seat.

As the bus started moving, Caleb whispered, "I don't want to go to school."

"You'll be fine," Jorah whispered back.

"My tummy hurts," said Caleb, rubbing his stomach.

Mora tapped a finger on Jorah's shoulder. "I thought he looked a little green," she said.

"You've got green on the brain," snapped Jorah as she put an arm around Caleb.

In the classroom Mrs. Postal started her lesson. "What's in a name?" she asked. "The month of August comes from the emperor Augustus Caesar, who was both the grandnephew of Julius Caesar and the first emperor of Rome. Does anyone know why Augustus and Julius were given the name Caesar?"

Keira raised her hand. "I think I was named after a kaiser. Isn't that like an emperor? And isn't that the same as Caesar?"

"Yes, it is," said Mrs. Postal. "Very good. My first name is Anne, and I was named after my grandma Anna, who came from Russia. Anna means 'graceful' in Russian."

Kerry waved her hand. "Are you graceful, Mrs. Postal?"

"Not a bit!" Mrs. Postal laughed. "I'm a klutz like my grandfather." She picked up a book and leafed through its pages. "Ginger comes from the Latin *gingiber*, and it is also the name of a spice," she announced.

Ginger blushed until her cheeks matched her hair.

"Jay, your name comes from the Old French for *jaybird*," said Mrs. Postal.

Jay flapped his arms as if he were flying and started hooting like an owl.

"And Mora," said Mrs. Postal, "do you know what your name means?"

Mora said proudly, "It means 'little blueberry' in Spanish. My mother told me that a long time ago."

A tall girl with a swinging ponytail walked into the room and handed Mrs. Postal a note. Mrs. Postal read it and said, "Jorah, this young lady is here to take you to the office. Go along with her, dear."

Jorah's stomach did a somersault as she followed the swinging ponytail out the door. Why did she have to go to the office?

Perhaps her mother had broken her leg or something and needed Jorah at home. Perhaps her father hated his new job, and they were moving, right away, back to their old apartment. Perhaps Jorah's old school had written and told the principal that she should repeat her last grade.

It was silent in the hallway as Jorah and the ponytail rounded the corner. The only

sounds were the padding of the ponytail's sneakers and the squeak of Jorah's new green shoes. Jorah's stomach made one more flipflop, and then it dawned on her why she had to go to the office.

She would walk in the door, and the principal would stand behind her desk and point a bony finger at Jorah's feet. "There is a rule at Glen Forest School," the principal would boom. "None of my students is ever allowed to wear green shoes with green feathers on them. Ever, ever, ever!" Then the principal would shake her finger once, twice, three times, saying, "And that means you, you, you!"

Except that as they approached the principal's office, the ponytail sailed past it and made a right turn into the room marked "Nurse." Jorah followed her.

CHAPTER 4
JORAH AND CALEB

When Jorah entered the nurse's office, no bony fingers were pointed at her.

A lady in a blue smock was bent over a chair, holding a basin under the chin of a little boy. The top of his blond head, bent over the bowl, looked a lot like Caleb's.

The little boy was crying, and he sounded a lot like Caleb. The nurse continued to hold the basin until the little boy made a sharp noise and threw up into the bowl. Then the lady took a cloth and wiped the little boy's mouth.

The girl with the ponytail said, "Yuck!" and clamped two fingers around her nose.

The little boy spoke. "Is that you, Jorah? I'm sick."

"Caleb!" said Jorah, rushing forward.

"Here you are," said the nurse, nodding at the two girls. "You can go back to class, Kathy," she said to the ponytail, who left the room quickly. "Caleb is not a happy little boy right now," she said to Jorah, "and your mother doesn't seem to be home. I left her a message. Now why don't you take off his soiled shirt, and I'll go get him a smock to put on?"

Before Jorah could say a word, the nurse walked briskly out of the room. Jorah was left with a disgusting shirt whose football design was covered with something that she wouldn't touch in science class.

She wrinkled up her nose and carefully rolled the shirt up to her brother's armpits. "Pull your hands out of the sleeves," she instructed Caleb, but Caleb just sat there with his arms out like a scarecrow's and tears running down his face.

"I don't feel good, Jorah," he said, making the same terrible sound that Jorah had heard a minute before.

Jorah looked around for the basin, but it was gone, so she grabbed the wastepaper basket and held it under her brother's chin the way she'd seen the nurse do it.

Caleb threw up into the basket and dipped his head down until it was almost inside. "Thank you, Jorah," he whispered. "I feel a little better now."

"It's okay, honey," said Jorah, making a second attempt to pull his shirt off.

The nurse bustled back into the office and, with a quick motion, rolled the shirt over Caleb's head and thrust it into a plastic bag. She tied the bag with a twisty and handed it to Jorah. "Hold this for when your mother comes, dear. And tell her to open it with care." Then she slipped Caleb's arms into the sleeves of a clean blue smock.

Just then Mama ran into the office. "I was at the supermarket, and I got here as fast as I could," she said breathlessly.

"He's feeling a little better now," said Jorah.

"Sweetheart," said Mama, sitting next to Caleb and shifting him like a sack of potatoes onto her lap.

"Your daughter was a big help," said the

nurse, carrying the wastebasket out the door. "There's a stomach bug going around," she called over her shoulder. "Rest and flat ginger ale."

"I don't like ginger ale," Caleb said to his mother.

"He likes cream soda," said Jorah.

"Cream soda won't settle his stomach," said Mama, sliding Caleb off her lap. "Can you walk, honey? The car's right outside."

"Bye, Jorah," said Caleb, shuffling ahead of his mother out the door. "I told you I didn't want to go to school."

"Thank you, Jorah," said Mama, kissing her on the top of the head.

Jorah handed her mother the bag. "Don't forget this," she said. "It's pretty gross."

Jorah walked back down the hallway to room number eight. She sighed and sniffed her hands. There was no way she was going to walk back into her classroom smelling like poor Caleb.

Jorah entered the bathroom marked "Girls," squeezed some soap into her hands

from the dispenser, and scrubbed hard. She looked into the mirror. Her face was pale and serious. She had no real friends. Her brother was at home with her mother, drinking ginger ale and eating toast and watching television. Her birthday was only two days away, and there was no one, absolutely no one, to celebrate it.

Back in her classroom Jorah slipped into her chair and hoped that no one smelled anything but soap and water.

"Is everything okay, Jorah?" said Mrs. Postal.

"My brother was sick," said Jorah.

"I told you," said Mora. "He looked sick in the bus," she told the class. "He looked like he was going to barf then and there."

"Thank you, Mora," said Mrs. Postal above the groans of the children. "Just what we wanted to hear, now that it's lunchtime. I hope he gets better soon, Jorah. It was nice that you could help."

After school Jorah boarded the bus to go home. She took the empty seat next to somebody she didn't know, so that Mora couldn't sit by her. Mama was waiting at the bus stop, holding Caleb's hand.

"Let's get home quickly," she said to Jorah. "I don't want Caleb to catch a chill."

Jorah followed her mother the few blocks home and watched as she settled Caleb on the couch. "Could I have crackers?" said Caleb wanly.

"I guess so," said Mama. "You're getting your appetite back."

"I'll have some crackers and peanut butter," said Jorah, who noted that her mother gave Caleb his crackers first.

Jorah went up to her room. She checked the wall for crickets. Then she took out her felt-tipped pen, opened up her journal, and wrote:

Today is the second worst day of my life. We learned about names today. We didn't get to my name because Caleb was sick and I had to go help him. It was gross. Now Mama is giving him all the attention. If Mora means blueberry, she needs to be squished. If Jay means jaybird, I wish he would fly away. Today is the second worst day of my life, because in two more days it will be the worst. My birthday, the day I was born, and no party. I miss my old school, and I miss my old friends. The end.

CHAPTER 5
JORAH'S BIRTHDAY

On the morning of Jorah's birthday Mama made pancakes for breakfast. Papa put candles on them, and the whole family sang "Happy Birthday to You."

When Mama walked Caleb and Jorah to the bus stop, Jorah carefully carried a tray of homemade chocolate cupcakes for the entire class to eat.

"Is it your birthday?" asked Mora as she stepped behind Jorah.

"Yes," said Jorah, smiling at Mora for the very first time.

"You should have told me," said Mora.

"I helped ice the cupcakes," Caleb said proudly.

Mora looked surprised. "Weren't you sick to your stomach yesterday?" she asked.

"He was better by yesterday afternoon," Jorah said quickly as the school bus pulled over to the curb.

"I hope so," said Mora, climbing up the steps behind her. "Otherwise, nobody is going to want to eat them."

But Jorah noticed at snack time that Mora was the first person to grab a cupcake. Jay called them "lumpcakes" instead of "cupcakes" because of Caleb's

uneven icing, but he had one anyway. Ginger and Kerry wished her happy birthday and ate their cupcakes in the corner.

Mrs. Postal gave her a shiny new pencil with "Glen Forest School" written on it.

"Happy birthday, Jorah," she said. "You have such a pretty name, you know, and it wasn't listed in my book. Will you tell us about it tomorrow?"

Jorah said she would, and asked Mrs. Postal if she could write down what Caleb's name meant.

Mrs. Postal handed Jorah a slip of paper. "It has two meanings," she said. "He'll like one, and not the other."

Melissa waved her hand wildly and said, "You forgot about me!"

Mrs. Postal turned to the "M" pages. "Melissa is Greek and means 'honeybee' or 'honey,'" she announced.

Jay and Calvin made buzzing sounds until Mrs. Postal shushed them. "Calvin, your name means 'bald' in Latin, so your mother had you pegged all wrong! Look at that head of hair!"

Calvin shook his mop of hair and took a bow. "I was bald when I was born," he explained, so Jay called him Baldy for the rest of the day.

It was raining when Jorah left school. She got soaked getting on and off the bus, and she forgot her math notebook, which made her mother yell. Then Jorah told Caleb that his name meant "dog" in Hebrew, which made him cry and made her mother yell some more.

Jorah went up to her bedroom. She changed into some dry clothes and sat down at her desk. On the blotter lay a card from Caleb that said "Caleb Love Jorah" in five-year-old handwriting. Jorah moved it aside and wrote:

Let me tell you about the worst birthday ever. Caleb is a crybaby and Mom is grouchy and Dad is late for dinner and so is my cake.

Rain clattered noisily on the rooftop. Jorah looked out her window at the street below.

The girl in the blue rain slicker whom Jorah had seen on moving day was dancing in the puddles. Autumn leaves were doing a dance of their own.

Jorah watched wistfully as the girl twirled her daisy umbrella. She wished with all her heart that she was dancing and singing in the rain with Sami, back in her old world.

The doorbell rang. Jorah ran down the stairs and swung open the door. Standing outside was a wet little girl in a blue rain slicker holding a daisy umbrella.

"Happy birthday," said a voice that sounded familiar, as she handed Jorah a package with a bow on it that matched her raincoat.

"Come in," said Jorah, stepping aside.

"Will you stay for some cake?" said Mama, joining them.

The little girl nodded and said, "I'll just call my mother."

Jorah took the girl's wet umbrella and put it in the umbrella stand. "Meet my new friend Mora," she said to her mother.

"It means 'little blueberry' in Spanish," said Mora.

"And it rhymes with Jorah," said Jorah.

The two girls smiled at each other.

"Do you remember what Jorah means?" said Mama.

"Yes," said Jorah. "But you tell us anyway."

Mama said, "When you were born, I held you in my arms and listened to the rain outside my window. And Grandma told me it was good luck and to call you Jorah."

Mora smiled. "So it means 'good luck'?"

Mama shook her head. "It means 'autumn rain' in Hebrew."

Mora said, "Now you really have to open your present," so Jorah unwrapped her present and took out a brand-new daisy umbrella.

Then Jorah and Mora went dancing in the rain, twirling their matching daisy umbrellas

That night, after the family and Mora

had dinner and cake and blew out the candles and sang "Happy Birthday to You," Jorah sat down at her desk. She didn't bother to check the walls for crickets. She opened up her journal and wrote:

I played in the rain with my new friend Mora. Mama told me that Jorah means autumn rain in Hebrew. That's good because I love the rain. My teacher says that Caleb means dog in Hebrew, but it also means heart. I'll tell Caleb in the morning. He'll like that much better. Today Caleb told me that his new world is good. So is mine. Tomorrow after school I'm playing at Mora's house. The day after that she's coming here. I'll write all about it—if I have time.